NOTHING
BUT NET

TEXT BY NATASHA DEEN
ILLUSTRATED BY KATIE WOOD

Raintree is an imprint of Capstone Global Library Limited, a company
incorporated in England and Wales having its registered office at 264 Banbury
Road, Oxford, OX2 7DY – Registered company number: 6695582

www.raintree.co.uk
myorders@raintree.co.uk

Originated by Capstone Global Library Ltd
Printed and bound in the United Kingdom

978 1 3982 0430 0

British Library Cataloguing in Publication Data
A full catalogue record for this book is available from the British Library.

CONTENTS

CHAPTER 1

SWISH!

"Swing, batter, batter, swing!"

Layla Safar chuckled as she faced off against the other girl on the basketball court. "This is basketball, not baseball," she said.

"Give me a break," Danika grinned. She pushed her blonde hair off of her forehead. Danika took the triple-threat stance opposite Layla. "I spent the summer with my family in Europe," she said. "I'm rusty."

"I'm not!" Layla dribbled down the court towards the net. She took her shot. *Swish!*

The ball fell through. "Yes!" Layla pumped her fist.

Danika caught the ball. "That was amazing!"

Layla blushed with pleasure. Danika was one of the best players on their basketball team, the Green Meadows Wolves.

"Thanks," said Layla. "I've spent most of my summer at camp and been practising every day."

"It shows," said Danika. "You'll make the team again."

"Last year I was a substitute," said Layla. "This year, I want to be a starter." She smiled. "Like you."

Danika grimaced. "I don't know if I'll even make the team. I didn't practise at all this summer."

"You'll make it," said Layla. She moved back to the centre line and crouched into position.

Danika mirrored her stance. "I still can't believe we lost to the Wildcats last year."

"We'll beat them this season," Layla promised.

Danika grabbed the ball from Layla. She faked going left, then sprinted down the court.

Layla chased after her. She got in front of Danika. As Danika went for the basket, Layla jumped and batted the ball from her friend's hands.

Layla grabbed it and moved to the other net. Time for her lay-up shot! Left foot, right foot, release the ball. It went in!

"Awesome!" Danika tossed her the ball. "My turn."

Layla dribbled the ball down centre court. Danika ran to the net. Layla passed the ball to Danika, who caught it, took the shot, and made the basket.

"Nice!" said Danika. She threw the ball to Layla.

The honk of a car horn pulled them from their fun.

"It's my mum," said Danika. "Do you want a lift home?"

"Thanks," said Layla. "My dad's working late at the hospital today."

"We're going to rock try-outs," Danika assured her friend.

Layla gave her a high five. "I agree!"

CHAPTER 2

MAKING THE CUT

The final class bell rang on Tuesday afternoon, and Layla sped to the gym locker room. It buzzed with nervous chatter.

Violet, one of the girls from last year's team, came over. "I hope I make the cut again." She grimaced. "And I hope I don't pull my tendon during finals this time."

"Is your foot okay now?" asked Layla.

Violet nodded. "I think so," she said.

Layla spotted Sydney. "No way! Sydney, are you trying out this year?"

Sydney finished her plait and came over. "You had so much fun last year. I had to try. Besides, I spend all my time playing with you guys at the park or at your house. I might as well become part of the team."

"That's awesome," said Layla. "Good luck!"

"Come on, slowpokes," Danika called. "Let's go!"

Everyone headed out of the locker room and into the gym. The floor was polished and shiny, and the lines for the basketball court were freshly painted and bright. Coach Okar and Assistant Coach Greenberg were waiting.

Layla's heart tripped with excitement. This was the moment she'd spent all summer practising for, and it was finally here!

"Gather around!" Coach Okar called. "It's great to see everyone. We're looking for players who love the game and their team. We're going to push you to give your best because we're going to go to finals this year!"

The girls cheered.

"Give me ten laps!" said Assistant Coach Greenberg.

Layla ran as fast as she could. She finished her final lap and sprinted back. Danika was already done. Sydney and Violet were still running.

"Hurry up!" Danika called. "Go faster!"

Layla cheered for her friends. "Keep going, Sydney! You got this, Violet!"

"Good work," said Assistant Coach Greenberg when the last girl finished.

"Now the swish drill," he continued. "Three players to the free-throw line, three to the left of the net, and three to the right."

The girls took their spots.

"I want each of you to make a basket," Assistant Coach Greenberg said. "But no bouncing the ball off the backboard, and no hitting the rim. We're looking for proper shooting form. Nothing but net, okay?"

"Keep trying until you get that swish sound," added Coach Okar.

Danika got her shot on the first try.

"Way to go!" Layla cheered.

It was Sydney's turn. The ball bounced off the backboard.

"No worries," called Layla. "Next time!"

Sydney tried again. On her third try, the ball went in.

"I knew you could do it!" Layla cheered.

My turn, thought Layla. She got it on the first try. She grinned. Last year, it had taken her three tries.

Try-outs continued with the coaches running two-on-two plays and passing drills.

By the time Coach Okar blew the final whistle, Layla's shirt was soaked with sweat and her legs felt like jelly. Her lay-ups had been soft and she'd fouled Violet during one of the plays, but Layla was proud of herself.

"Let's grab some ice cream," said Danika after they'd changed.

The girls headed out, but as they stepped into the sunny day, Layla said, "Oh no! I forgot my backpack." She ran back to the locker room and got her bag. On her way out, she walked by the coaches' office.

She heard Coach Okar say, "It needs to be Layla."

"I agree," said Assistant Coach Greenberg.

Layla's heart thumped. *Oh no*, she thought. *Are they talking about who to cut?* Layla ran to Danika. She told Danika what she'd overheard.

"They're probably talking about the substitute players," said Danika.

Layla was not convinced. *I tried so hard to make the starting five*, Layla thought as she fought back her tears. *I can't believe I'm subbing again.*

Danika looked worried, so Layla forced a smile and said, "Let's go and get that ice cream!"

CHAPTER 3

AN UNEXPECTED PLAY

On Friday afternoon, the girls were at the gym, watching anxiously as Coach Okar posted the team roster.

"To those of you who didn't make the cut," Coach said, "don't be too disappointed. Practise, learn and come back next year."

Layla read the seven names on the sub list. Her name wasn't there, but she was happy to see that her friend Rebecca Jefferson had made the team. Layla moved to the starting-five names.

Danika Ivanov, centre.

Keana Cardinal, power forward.

Sydney Lancaster, small forward.

Violet Kim, shooting guard.

Layla Safar, point guard, captain.

"Captain?" Layla whispered. "I made captain?"

"You made captain!" Sydney yelled and grabbed her in a hug.

"I can't believe it!" Layla said. She looked for Danika but didn't see her.

"Believe it," said Coach Okar. "We were impressed by your try-out."

"But there are other players who are better than me," said Layla.

"It's not just the skills that make the captain," said Coach Okar. "It's about a person's ability to create a team environment."

Coach continued, "During try-outs, you encouraged your teammates. That's the heart of a leader, and that's why you've been made captain."

Layla thanked Coach Okar, and then ran to find Danika.

She was at her locker.

"We made the team!" Layla hugged her friend.

"We did," said Danika. She didn't sound happy.

Layla pulled away. "What's wrong?"

"When you overheard the coaches talking about you, did you know they were going to make you captain?" asked Danika. "Did you keep a secret from me?"

"Never!" said Layla. "I was afraid I was getting cut."

"You're too good to get cut," Danika said. "They made you captain."

Danika seemed grumpy, so Layla didn't talk about how excited and nervous she was to be made team captain. Instead, she said, "Practice is on Monday and Thursday. Do you want to come over for dinner on those days?"

Danika shrugged. "I guess."

"Sydney, Keuna and Violet made the starting five too. Isn't that awesome?" said Layla.

Danika nodded.

The girls walked home in silence.

She's not being fair, Layla thought. *We both made the starting five. I get she's upset she didn't make captain, but I thought she'd be happy for me.*

When they got to Layla's house, Layla invited Danika inside.

"No, thanks," said Danika. "I should get home." She waved and walked away.

Later that night, Danika texted Layla: *Sorry I was a downer. I'm happy we made the team, but I hoped I would get the captain's spot.*

Layla typed her response: *TY 4 apologizing. I get you're disappointed.*

Danika replied: *Yeah, but YOU MADE CAPTAIN! ^_^ That's awesome! I'm sorry I was jealous! I promise I'll be a better friend and teammate.*

Layla sighed in relief. She and Danika were back to normal. Now Layla could focus on being a great captain.

CHAPTER 4

CAPTAIN ON THE COURT

On Monday, Layla's dad dropped her off at school. "Go get 'em, captain!" he said. "How about spaghetti for you and Danika tonight?"

"Sounds yummy! Love you!" She waved goodbye and walked to her school locker.

"Ready for practice?" Danika asked as she came up to Layla.

"Not really," admitted Layla. "I'm nervous. I tried texting you a few times this weekend, but you never responded."

Danika shrugged. "I was busy practising. Everyone's got really good over the summer, and I need to catch up."

"I would have helped," said Layla.

"Thanks, Captain," said Danika, "but I've got this." Danika smiled, but Layla was sure there was a frown hidden behind the smile.

"Let's get to lessons," said Danika.

"Are you sure you're okay with me being captain?" Layla asked.

"Promise," said Danika. "Come on, let's go!"

* * *

"Move to the next drill!" Coach Okar called to the players.

Layla lined up with her team. Each of them had a ball. Crouching low, Layla got into position with the ball in her right hand.

FWEET! Coach blew her whistle.

Layla walked forward and threaded the ball between her legs. She caught it with her left hand and rolled the ball again. Layla moved quickly and was the first one to the other side.

Violet was second. "Nice job!" she said.

"You too!" Layla said. She watched the team but concentrated on Danika. She was one of the last to finish. Danika saw Layla. She scowled and turned away.

After the warm-ups, Assistant Coach Greenberg broke the team into groups for three-on-three drills. Layla partnered with Danika and Sydney. They got into position opposite Violet, Keana and one of the subs, Rebecca.

Assistant Coach Greenberg blew his whistle and threw the ball to Rebecca. She handed it off to Violet. The game was on!

Violet dribbled down the paint, but Layla batted the ball from her opponent's hand.

Pivoting, she spotted Danika and passed the ball.

Danika caught it and dribbled down the lane. She took a jump shot but missed the net.

Layla caught it on the rebound and went for the shot. She made the basket!

Keana grabbed the ball and the girls regrouped. This time, Layla moved along the court. Keana spotted Rebecca and passed her the ball.

Rebecca took the shot. It went in!

Sydney caught the ball. She dribbled down the lane and passed to Danika, who went for a jump shot. The ball bounced off the rim.

Layla caught it just as the coach blew the

final whistle.

"Good work," she said. "Before you leave, we have news. The Cherry Orchard Wildcats have invited us to a friendly game. It will be in three weeks."

"They cut us out of the finals last year," Layla said. "Let's show them we're coming hard this season."

The team shouted in agreement.

"I hoped you'd say that," said Coach Okar. "Great practice, everyone. See you on Thursday!"

Layla was covered in sweat, but she felt great. The team was trying hard. With a little work, they would beat the Wildcats. She changed and went to find Danika.

Danika was with Violet and Sydney. They were heading to the door.

"Hang on!" Layla hurried to her friends.

"We were talking about our weak spots," said Danika. "My shots on the net are rough."

"My dribbling isn't great," said Sydney.

"Concentrate on using the pads of your fingers to dribble, Sydney," said Layla.

She nodded.

"Danika, if you let the ball roll off your fingertips, it'll help your shots," said Layla.

"I know," said Danika. "I wish my muscles knew it too." The girls laughed.

"There's my dad," said Layla. "Ready for dinner, Danika? He's making spaghetti."

"Oh no!" said Danika. "I forgot about hanging out after practice! My mum's already here. Next time?"

Layla smiled. "Deal."

CHAPTER 5

WHO WANTS A TROPHY?

After dinner, Layla went to her room. She created a group text for her and the other eleven players on the Wolves team. Layla typed:

*Who wants a trophy? ;-) Extra practice at my house, every Wednesday (if you can make it) until the season is over. My dad says he'll provide snacks. ^_^*

Sydney: *YASSSSS!*

Violet: *I'll B there!*

Danika: *Wildcats = trophy = I'll B there, Captain!*

Eventually, all of the team texted and most girls could make the extra practice. Layla hugged the phone. She ran downstairs to tell her dad the good news.

* * *

"That's a foul!" Sydney laughed as Danika grabbed her by the waist and stopped her from taking the shot.

"It looks like fair play to me," Violet said. "Danika, get the ball. Pass it my way!"

It was Wednesday afternoon and the team was playing pick-up at the basketball court by Layla's house. Layla giggled as Keana jumped on Danika, and the rest of the team piled on.

We have a great time together, Layla thought. *I hope basketball is always this much fun.*

"Come on, Captain!" Danika laughed. "Save me!"

"Time to be serious," Layla said as she pulled Danika to her feet. "Let's practise our plays. Get into position for the ghost play!"

The girls took their spots.

"Go!" As Layla passed the ball to Danika, Violet ran to the left side of the net. Sydney ran to the right.

Layla sped to the paint and positioned herself in front of the net. Danika threw the ball to Layla. She quickly passed it to Sydney, who took a shot. The ball bounced off the backboard, and Layla caught it for the rebound. She arced the ball into the net!

"Brilliant!" said Layla. "Let's try that again. We're a bit slow."

The girls regrouped and reran the play.

"We're still slow," said Danika. "Sydney, you need to be more aggressive."

Sydney nodded.

"One more time, team!" said Layla.

They repeated the play.

"It's still not working," Danika growled. "We're too slow."

"Let's grab some water. Then we can try again," Layla said.

"No breaks," said Danika. "We need to keep going."

Layla agreed to try, but even a fourth time didn't help. "Let's break this into drills," she said. "We'll work it out, step-by-step."

Danika scowled. "The Wildcats aren't going to stop a game for us to run a drill. We have to push hard."

"Playing when we're exhausted doesn't help anyone," said Layla.

"Don't you want us to be ready for finals?" Danika asked.

"Yes, but–"

"So, let's run the play again," snapped Danika.

"We haven't had a break!" Layla snapped back. She noticed the other girls looked worried. *We've had such a good time,* she thought, *I don't want to ruin it.*

"Let's grab some water," Layla said to Danika. "We'll try another play. Maybe we need a break from this one. I'll think about what you said. Maybe we should be pushing harder."

Danika nodded.

"Anyone need a snack?" Dr Safar walked up to them with a basket filled with muffins.

"Good timing, Dad," said Layla. "We're just taking a break."

CHAPTER 6

PERSONAL FOUL

The next day, Layla found Coach Okar in her office.

"There's my captain," said the coach. "You're doing a great job."

"I wish Danika could hear that," Layla sighed. "She doesn't think I'm pushing the team hard enough. I'm worried she's right, and I'm not being a good leader."

"*Is* she right?" Coach Okar asked.

"Keana's great, but Sydney could go harder," Layla admitted.

She continued, "And Violet is too timid sometimes. She also worries about getting hurt."

"Pretend you're the coach," said Coach Okar. "What would you do?"

"Our game against the Wildcats is only a friendly," Layla said. "It won't count towards the season or our rankings. If we go too hard, too fast, we can risk losing a player to injury. We should go slow and steady."

"That's the call I would make too," said Coach Okar in agreement.

Layla breathed in relief. If that's what Coach would do, then it was the right call.

* * *

At Monday's practice, the coaches warmed the team up with stretches and laps.

"Time for around-the-world drills," Coach Okar said. The phone in the office rang. "Layla," she said. "Take the lead while I answer the phone." She walked to the office.

"Hold your ball," Layla said to the team. "Wrap it around your head in a circle, then around your waist, your ankles. Then back up, again." Layla demonstrated. "Fast as you can, but don't drop the ball. Go!"

Layla watched her teammates. "Good job, Violet," she said.

Sydney dropped the ball, and it bounced off Danika's foot.

"Watch it," growled Danika.

"Sorry," said Sydney. She tried again to spin the ball around her head, but lost her grip. The ball bounced into Danika's shoulder.

Danika scowled at her teammate. "Losing control of the ball is going to cost us games," she said.

"It was an accident. Getting angry won't help," said Layla.

"You're the captain," Danika said. "You should be pushing Sydney. You said you agreed with me that we should be working harder."

"I said I'd think about it," said Layla. "But it doesn't work for the team."

"More like it doesn't work for you," said Danika. "You don't want to listen to anyone but yourself."

"What?" Layla cried. "Take that back!"

"Girls." Coach Okar came into the gym. "Is there a problem?"

"No," said Danika. "No problem."

"Good. Fall in line," said the coach. "Let's practise foul shots."

Layla moved close to Danika. She hoped they'd have a chance to talk about their argument. But Danika wouldn't look at her.

Layla noticed that when Danika took her shot, she was having trouble getting her ball to arc properly. "Do you want some help?" she asked. "I know a good tip."

"I don't need your help," Danika said. "I'm taking it slow and steady, just like you said." She walked away.

Layla blinked away the tears. *I don't know why she's being so mean,* she thought. *I'm just trying to help.*

After practice, Layla waited for Danika so they could go home together. But when Danika came out of the locker room, she passed by without looking at Layla.

CHAPTER 7

A ROUGH NIGHT

Layla texted Danika later that night, but she didn't reply. The next day, Danika wasn't waiting for her at their school locker. When Layla finally saw her in class, Danika gave her a half-hearted wave, but she didn't come over.

By Wednesday, Layla was heartbroken. This season was supposed to be the best ever. But here she was, eating lunch without her best friend. *Maybe I should cancel today's practice at the house,* she thought. *Where's the fun without Danika?*

As though reading her thoughts, Sydney came over. "Are we still meeting today? I've been working on my drills."

"Tell me we're practising after school," said Violet, as she and Keana walked over. "I've been working on my lay-ups."

As she listened to her friends, Layla went from sad to mad. She thought, *Everyone is working hard on the team, except Danika.*

Layla pulled out her phone. "I'm texting everyone," she said. She typed *practice @ my place 2day!* and hit *send.* Soon, everyone had replied with, *YES!*

Everyone but Danika.

Fine with me, thought Layla.

* * *

"Hurry up, everyone! I've been waiting forever!" Danika waved as the team gathered.

Layla stopped in surprise. "I didn't think you were coming," she said. "You never texted back."

"Of course I was coming," said Danika. "I'm on the team, aren't I? Why don't we warm up with some laps?" Danika suggested.

Is she trying to take over practice? Layla wondered, but she didn't say anything.

Danika came over. "I want to talk to you."

Talk? Layla questioned, *or argue?* "Later," she said. "We need to focus on the practice."

After they finished warming up, Sydney suggested starting practice with a game of around the world.

"I've got better at it," she said. She smiled at Danika. "It's safe to stand beside me."

Danika laughed.

"Okay, team, just like last time. Hold your ball," Layla said. "But this time, wrap it around your ankle in a circle, then around your waist, and then your head. Then back down again."

They started the drill with the balls at their ankles and worked their way up.

"You're doing great," Danika said to Sydney.

Sydney blushed with happiness.

Danika's trying to do my job, Layla thought.

"Good work!" said Layla. "Let's pick up the pace!" The team sped up the drill.

"Whoops!" Sydney's ball went sailing out of her hands and bounced on the tarmac. "Sorry!" She chased after it.

"Maybe we should slow down," said Danika.

"I thought you wanted us to push hard?" Layla shot back. "I'm doing what you want, aren't I?"

Violet, Keana and Sydney exchanged uncomfortable looks.

"Let's move on," said Layla. She had them work on their jump shots. Layla noticed Danika wasn't really trying.

"Put more power in your jump, Danika," Layla said. "We'll never get to finals if you can't shoot."

"I'm trying," Danika snapped.

"No, you're not," Layla snapped back. "You can't tell us to work hard, then not do it yourself."

"Don't get cross because I'm not perfect like you," shouted Danika.

"Don't yell at me!" Layla shot back.

"That's it!" Violet yelled. "I don't know what's up with you two, but sort it out!"

"I joined the team because you made it look like so much fun," said Sydney. "But this isn't fun at all." She and Violet walked away. The rest of the girls followed.

"I came today because we're a team and because you're my best friend," said Danika. She tucked her ball under her arm. "But mostly, I wanted to apologize for being an idiot. I thought we could work it out and I could help you with the captain stuff."

"I don't need your help," Layla said. "Coach Okar trusts me to make the calls."

"Funny," said Danika. "I thought between all the stuff you're doing, you'd find some time to be my friend."

She walked away and left Layla on the court, alone and fuming.

CHAPTER 8

DAD WITH THE ASSIST

Layla sat on the porch swing. She was still angry at Danika. Layla was captain, and she'd worked hard to earn the spot. And now, Danika's jealousy had ruined it.

Layla blinked back her tears. Losing her best friend felt terrible.

If it wasn't for Danika, I wouldn't even have tried out for the team last season, she thought.

Layla started to cry. She knew what she needed to do to fix her problem with Danika.

She went to find her dad. He was in the kitchen, stirring a pot of biryani rice. "Would you help with the salad?" he asked.

Layla took out a bag of vegetables from the fridge. "Dad? I think I'm going to stop being captain."

"Why?" he asked.

"It's making Danika and me fight. If I'm not captain, we'll be friends again," she said.

Dad stopped stirring the rice. "Why do you think you can't be friends with Danika and captain at the same time?"

Layla explained everything that had happened.

"I understand why you think stepping down will help," he said. "But in the end, it will only hurt your friendship."

"You and Danika won't stay the same people," he added. "There will be changes as you grow and try new things. Part of being a friend is working to make sure those changes make the friendship stronger."

Dad turned back to the pot of rice. "You're the captain, and Danika needs time to adjust to this. But you need to remember how she feels. She didn't get to play basketball this summer. I understand she feels like she has to push to catch up." He looked at her. "Do you?"

"I guess," answered Layla.

He smiled. "I know you're worried about your friendship, but I'm not. You and Danika care too much for each other and for basketball to lose either one. If you want to talk more, I'm here, okay?"

Layla nodded and wondered how to solve the rift between her and Danika.

CHAPTER 9

A TOUGH CONVERSATION

The next morning, Layla knocked on the door at Danika's house. As she waited, she listened to the thumping of her heart.

Danika opened the door. "What are you doing here?" she asked.

"We need to talk," Layla said. She took a breath. "When you turned up yesterday, I thought you were coming to embarrass me in front of the team. Then I got angry because I thought you were trying to take over my job. I was a bad friend and I'm sorry."

Danika gasped. "I'd never do that! I'm your friend!"

"But you haven't been acting like it," said Layla. "It feels like you're always mad at me."

"I know," said Danika. "That's why I came over yesterday. When I saw your text, I realized I hadn't been fair to you. I went to practice because I wanted to apologize. I haven't been a good friend, Layla. I'm sorry."

"That means a lot," said Layla.

Danika smiled. "I'm still struggling with feeling jealous, but not just with you. Everyone's got better. I feel like the weakest member of the team. I guess that's why I went overboard with pushing everyone."

"You're a little rusty because of the summer break," said Layla. "But you're an amazing player. You'll be running laps around me in no time."

"How are we going to work this out?" Danika asked. "I can't promise I won't get jealous or mad if I think you're not listening to me."

Layla sighed. "I can't promise I won't get frustrated, either. Dad says it'll take time for us to adjust to the changes in our friendship." She thought for a moment. "During the game, if the coaches need to talk to us, they call a time out. Maybe we can do the same thing."

"That's a good idea," said Danika. "We need a hand signal, though. I'd feel weird asking for a time out in front of the team."

"What about this?" Layla put her hand over her heart and tapped her chest twice.

Danika copied her. "Perfect." Danika grinned and nudged her. "As you're here, my basketball net could do with some practice."

Layla laughed. "I'm going to wipe the floor with you!"

"I'd like to see you try!" said Danika.

The girls ran to the driveway. Layla grinned. She felt good.

"Let's text the team," she said, smiling. "We owe them an apology for our argument yesterday."

Danika winced. "We do," she said. She pulled out her phone and started typing. *We're sorry for yesterday's fight. That wasn't cool of us. Practice at Danika's house. ~ Danika and Layla.*

The texts flooded in. The players accepted their apology and were heading over.

Layla gave Danika a high five. They were a team again – all of them.

CHAPTER 10

NOTHING BUT NET

FWEET! The referee blew his whistle and threw the ball in the air.

Layla caught it. She dribbled down the court.

The Wildcat guard blocked her.

Layla passed the ball to Violet who sent it to Sydney. She passed it to Danika who took a jump shot.

Swish! Nothing but net! Two points to the Wolves. *We're going to rock this,* Layla thought.

But by half-time, Layla wasn't so sure. The Cherry Orchard Wildcats had come back, hard. The score was 15–4. Wildcats were in the lead.

"This is terrible!" Sydney cried. She flopped on the locker room bench. "I don't mind losing, but they're wiping the floor with us!"

"We need to push harder," said Danika.

The team groaned.

"We're playing last year's champions!" she said.

The coaches came into the locker room.

"I know you're disappointed with the first half," said Coach Okar.

"But the game's not over yet," said Assistant Coach Greenberg. "We can still rally."

"To do that, we need to be clever. We need to switch up our plays and keep the Wildcats off guard," said Coach Okar.

She turned towards Layla. "When the whistle blows, Layla, I want you to pass to Violet, who'll get under the net. Violet, pass to Danika, who'll send the ball to Sydney. She'll go for the lay-up. Those of you guarding the Wildcats, I want you putting up your best screens."

"Grab a drink," said Assistant Coach Greenberg. "Layla, can we talk?"

Layla went with the coaches to a quiet corner.

"You're doing a great job," said Coach Okar. "But this is where your team will need you. They're feeling low. You need to encourage them."

"I don't know how," Layla said.

"Find a way," said Assistant Coach Greenberg. "Our plays won't help if the team thinks they've already lost the game."

They left Layla to come up with a plan.

Danika sat beside her. "I'm not wrong," she said. "We need to push harder."

"You saw us out there," Layla said. "We're playing as hard as we can."

"But–" Danika started to say.

"I can't talk right now," said Layla as she moved away. "I have to think." A few minutes later, she felt defeated. The second half was going to start, and Layla still didn't have a way to rally her team. She headed to the court with the players.

Her gaze caught Danika.

Danika lifted her hand to her heart and tapped twice.

Layla went over.

"Not all of us are playing as hard as we can," said Danika.

Keana overheard and blushed. "Sorry," she said.

"It's not just you," Danika said to Keana. Then she turned back to Layla. "Sydney is scared because it's her first real game as part of the team. Violet is holding back because she's afraid of getting hurt. But all of us play better when we're at your house—"

"That's it! Danika, you're a genius!" Layla ran to her teammates. "Listen up! We're taking everything too seriously. Sure, we want to win. But this is just a friendly game. It's just for fun. So let's just have a great time."

Layla put her hand on Sydney's shoulder. "I know it's scary to be on another team's turf, but you're doing an amazing job, okay?" She turned to Violet. "You're a great player, and you've got this."

The girls nodded.

The referee blew his whistle.

"Have fun out there!" Layla called.

Violet batted the ball from the Wildcats guard and passed it to Layla for a two-point shot. It went in!

The Wildcats brought the ball up the court. Danika intercepted a pass from a Wildcats forward and passed it to Layla for the shot. *Swish!* Basket!

The game continued until it was down to the last minute with the score tied at 17–17.

Layla took possession of the ball and sped towards the paint. Violet flanked her left. Layla deked around the Wildcats guard and passed the ball to Violet. She dribbled along the baseline.

Violet looped the ball around her waist and sent it to Danika. She passed the ball to Sydney, who banked the ball off the backboard and into the net.

The buzzer sounded. They'd won! The Wolves had eked out a win!

Danika hugged Layla. "Our coaches made the right call in making you captain. I couldn't have done what you did."

"But you helped," said Layla. "We're teammates and friends, forever! Come on, let's get the girls and grab some ice cream."

"Something with sprinkles," said Danika, "to celebrate our first – but not our last – win!"

About the Author

Natasha Deen loves stories – exciting ones, scary ones and especially funny ones! She lives in Edmonton, Alberta, Canada, with her family, where she spends a lot of time trying to convince her pets that she's the boss of the house.

About the Illustrator

Katie Wood fell in love with drawing when she was very small. Since graduating from Loughborough University School of Art and Design in 2004, she has been living her dream working as a freelance illustrator. From her studio in Leicester, she creates bright and lively illustrations for books and magazines all over the world.

GLOSSARY

anxious afraid or nervous about what may happen

flank to be on one side of an opponent or to alternate from one side to the other

pivot to turn while keeping one foot in place

position the place where a person or thing is or should be

ranking a listing of teams, from the team with the most amount of wins or points to the one with the least amount of wins or points

roster a list of people belonging to the same group or team

stance a way of standing

substitute to temporarily take someone else's place or position

tendon a band of tough body tissue that connects a muscle to a bone

timid to be shy or afraid

try-out a test of one's ability, such as with an athlete or actor, to fill a part or meet the necessary requirements

Discussion Questions

1. Layla spends her summer practising every day. Can you remember a time when you wanted to improve at a hobby or sport? What were some of the things you did to strengthen your skills?

2. When Violet and Sydney are having a hard time, Layla finds a way to encourage them. What are some other things she could have done to help her teammates?

3. At the Wednesday practice when Layla and Danika argue, the other girls on the team walk away. If you were there, would you have done the same thing? What other things could their teammates have done?

WRITING PROMPTS

1. Coach Okar tells Layla that one of the reasons they chose Layla for the position of captain is because she is supportive of her teammates. What other personality traits do you think the coaches were looking for in their players? Make a list.

2. Layla is surprised and delighted to make team captain. Have you ever had something unexpected and wonderful happen to you? Write what that experience was and how you felt.

3. Imagine you're playing in the game with the Wildcats. What plays might you have done in the final moments of the game?

More about Basketball

Basketball has some great words for players, the court and moves. Here are some terms to help you enjoy the game!

Basketball Glossary

DEKE

a move used to trick opponents; pretending to go one way, then going the other way

FOUL

when a player breaks a rule (usually by improper contact)

FOUL SHOT

an unguarded shot at the free-throw line

FREE-THROW LINE

a line fifteen feet from the basket, where a player stands to take a foul shot

LAY-UP

when a player shoots close to the hoop

PAINT/FREE-THROW LANE

the area underneath the net that is painted
in different colours from the rest of the court

REBOUND

when the ball bounces off of the backboard

SCREEN

when a player stands in front of their
opponent to block them

STARTER

one of the five players who are on the court
for the opening jump ball

SUBS

players that substitute in for starters

TRIPLE-THREAT STANCE

a player standing with their feet slightly
bent and shoulder-width apart

KEEP THE SPORTS ACTION GOING...